Tales
for Little
Children

Tales for Little Children

Contents

Goldilocks
and the
Three Bears

Once there was a little girl named Goldilocks.

She looked like a little angel...

...but she was really a little trouble maker.

She was naughty from first thing in the morning...

all through the day...

...to last thing at night.

And she never, ever did as she was told.

9

"Please go and get some bread from the village,"
said Goldilocks' mother one day.

"Go straight there," she added firmly.

"I will," sighed Goldilocks.

But Goldilocks soon
wandered off.

She saw smoke billowing from
the chimney of a thatched cottage.

"What a funny little house,"
she thought.

She pressed her face
against the window.

"No one at home," she
thought with a grin.

She pushed open the front
door, and a terrifically tasty
smell wafted out.

Goldilocks skipped inside.

There on a table were
three bowls of porridge.

Ahhhhh!

First she tried the
biggest bowl.

Her face flushed bright red.
"Too hot!" she gasped.

Then she tried the
middle-sized bowl.

"Ooo!" cried Goldilocks.
"Too cold!"

Last of all, she tried
the little bowl.

It was the yummiest
porridge she'd
ever tasted.

Slurp! Burp!

"What next?" she said.

In front of a crackling
fire were three chairs.

First, she tried
the biggest one.

"Too hard!" she said,
rubbing her sore bottom.

Then she tried the
middle-sized one.

16

"Too soft!" yelped Goldilocks, sinking into the squishy cushions.

She sat down firmly on the smallest chair.

But seconds later came a *snap!*

and the little wooden chair collapsed.

"I need a nap," yawned Goldilocks.

She climbed the stairs...

and came to a big, bright bedroom.

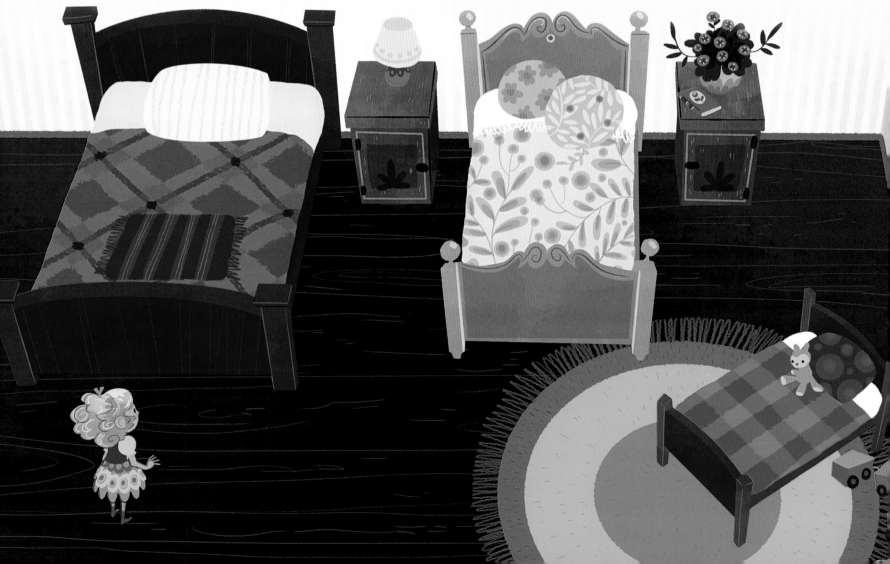

First, she tried
the biggest bed.

"Too high!" she puffed,
out of breath.

Then she tried the
middle-sized bed.

"Too deep!" she cried,
drowning in the
squashy mattress.

Help!

Last of all, she tried the smallest bed.

She climbed on top and rested her head on the soft, downy pillow.

"Ah," she said. "Just right."

Pulling the blankets up to her chin, she snuggled down and fell asleep.

Meanwhile, the owners of the house returned.

"Who left the front door open?" asked Father Bear.

"Not me, dear," said Mother Bear.

"Not me," echoed Baby Bear.
They went inside.

"Hey! Someone's been eating my porridge," grumbled Father Bear.

"Someone's been eating *my* porridge,"
sighed Mother Bear.

"And someone's been eating *my* porridge,"
sniffed Baby Bear, "and they've eaten it **all** up!"

Worse was to come...

"Someone's been sitting in my chair!"
exclaimed Father Bear.

"Someone's been sitting in *my* chair,"
added Mother Bear.

"And someone's been sitting in *my* chair," wailed Baby Bear, "and they've **broken** it to pieces!"

Just then, they heard snoring.

The three bears followed the noise upstairs...

What a mess!

"Someone's been sleeping in my bed," boomed Father Bear.

"Someone's been sleeping in *my* bed," gasped Mother Bear.

"Someone's been sleeping in *my* bed," squealed Baby Bear...

"...and she's still in it!"

Goldilocks woke with a start to find
three grumpy bears glaring at her.

She leaped from the bed,
scrambled downstairs,
and raced outside.

She didn't stop running until she got home.

"I'm really sorry for not doing what I was told," Goldilocks said to her mother.

"I promise I'll never, ever be naughty again."

And she never was...

...well, *almost* never!

Tom Thumb

Thomas and Eve really, *really* wanted a child.

Finally, Eve decided to ask Merlin the Magician.

"We really, *really* want a child," she said sweetly.
"Please?"

Even one the
size of a thumb!

Ho hum, size of a thumb...

Abracadabracadoo!

33

As if by magic, Eve had a baby boy...

...and he *was* the size of a thumb.

Eve made him...

a cobweb
top,

feather
shorts,

apple-skin
shoes

and an oak
leaf hat.

Let's call him
Tom Thumb!

It wasn't easy
being so small.

Tom was always getting lost.

Guess where he turned up on market day?

SURPRISE!

There's danger everywhere when you're small.

YUM
YUM!

"Tom? Where are you?"

BURRRP!

"That was a close escape!"

Little Tom couldn't even scare a crow.

Shoo!

One day, he was trying his best, when a crow rudely *swooped* him away...

Let me go!

...and dropped him in a lake.

SPLOSH!

That same day, a fisherman caught a fish.

The fish was served
on a silver dish...

...and the dish was served
to the King.

SURPRISE!

44

The King liked Tom Thumb.

I'm an excellent pea juggler.

Merlin and the knights liked Tom Thumb.

I can fight off
fearsome flies.

"I'll make you a knight, too!" announced the King.

And so Tom Thumb became *Sir* Tom
– the smallest knight in the kingdom.

Sir Tom hunted down spiders...

CHARGE!

chased after dragonflies...

HALT!

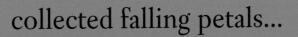
collected falling petals...

DON'T
PANIC!

...and saved
drowning moths.

49

The King rewarded his little knight
with a shiny gold coin.

"Thank you, Sire!" said Tom.
"But now I think it's time to go home."

Sir Tom bid farewell to his castle friends and set off home.

Thomas and Eve were delighted to see him.

"I've brought you a coin from the King!" he cried.

Tom told his parents about the crow and the fish,
the peas and the petals, the spiders and the dragonflies.

"It's fun being the size of a thumb," said Tom.

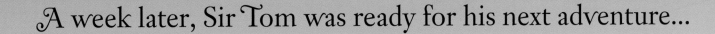

A week later, Sir Tom was ready for his next adventure...

Be careful, Tom!

Don't worry,
I always am.

The Genie in the Bottle

Once upon a time, a fisherman went fishing.

He cast his net over
the foaming waves.

He caught tangles
of slimy seaweed,

handfuls of
shiny shells

Urgh!

and someone's
stinky old sock...

...but not one fish.

He cast his net once more.
This time, he felt something
heavy.

"It must be a fish,"
he thought, hauling it in.

"A really BIG fish!"

But it wasn't.

It was a tall glass bottle, its sides misty with age.

Why was it so heavy?

Pop! He pulled out the stopper and peeked in...

"Empty!" he exclaimed in surprise.

Disappointed,
he let it drop.

CLUNK!

All at once, smoke began bubbling out of the top, billowing and blowing into strange shapes...

...until the fisherman found himself staring at a gigantic face.

"Uh-oh," he thought. "A genie!"

The genie's tummy growled and the genie scowled.
He stared hungrily at the fisherman.

"I need something to eat," he announced.
"I think I'll start with... YOU!"

The fisherman frowned.

"That's no way to behave," he said.
"After all, I just set you free."

You should
thank me!

"Ha!" snarled the genie. "I'm starving!
I've been stuck inside that rotten
bottle for far too long."

The fisherman thought fast.

"You were INSIDE this little bottle?" he snorted.

"A great big genie like you? I don't believe it!"

"YES!" snapped
the genie. "I was!"

"You're far too large," laughed the fisherman. "You'd never fit!"

"Watch this," huffed the genie.

Whooosh!

He whooshed back inside.

74

As the last wisp of smoke vanished,
the fisherman jammed in the stopper.

You can stay there
until you've learned
a little kindness!

Grrr!

Then the fisherman
went back to his fishing...

...and caught
a fine fresh fish
for dinner.

The
Stonecutter

There was once a penniless stonecutter.

He groaned and he griped
and he grumbled... all day long.

I'm tired.

This stone is
too hard.

A mountain spirit was passing by and saw him looking glum.

"Hmm..." thought the spirit.

83

That afternoon, a wealthy merchant bought some stone.

The stonecutter carried it to the merchant's magnificent mansion.

What a house!

The mountain spirit heard him.
He smiled and tapped his stick...

TAP!

TAP!

TAP!

And, lo and behold,
the stonecutter *was* rich.

He lazed on a lounger in the sun.

Ahh... This is the life!

"It's so wonderfully warm," he said
happily. "I wish I was the sun."

The mountain spirit heard him.
He smiled and waved his arms...

FIZZ!

BANG!

WHOOSH!

KAZAM!

The stonecutter was the sun.

He shone down with joy.
Flowers bloomed and
everyone beamed.

The stonecutter turned up
the heat. He blasted his rays.

Flowers wilted
and turned brown.

The river dried up
and cracked.

Now people frowned.

"Well, this is no fun,"
said the stonecutter sun.

To everyone's delight,
it began to rain.
Raindrops soaked into
the parched ground.

"I wish I was a raincloud,"
the stonecutter declared.

The mountain spirit heard him.
He smiled and zapped his finger...

ZAPPETY-ZAP!

...and the stonecutter was a raincloud.

The stonecutter began to rain.

Splish! Splash! Splosh!

Oh no! He couldn't **stop** raining.

Soon, the ground was flooded.

Water covered everything... except a grassy mountain.
"I wish I was a mountain," he moaned.

The mountain spirit heard him.
He smiled and pointed his stick...

ZAP! The stonecutter was a mountain.
"This is more like it," thought the stonecutter with a grin.
"Being a mountain is so peaceful... HEY!"

Another stonecutter had strolled up
and was cutting chunks out of him.

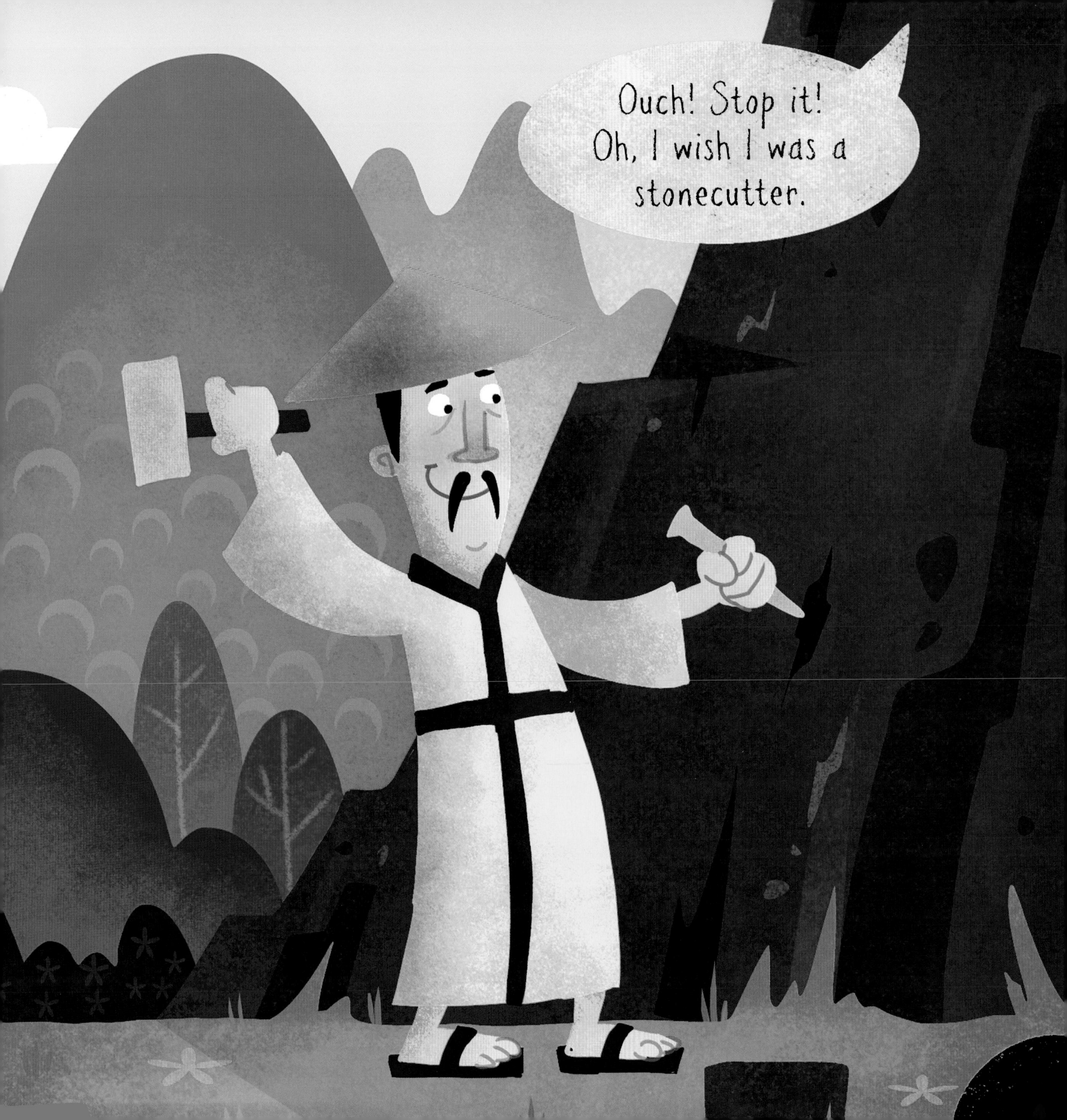
Ouch! Stop it! Oh, I wish I was a stonecutter.

The mountain spirit heard him.
He smiled down one last time...

KAZAM!

The stonecutter was back where he started.

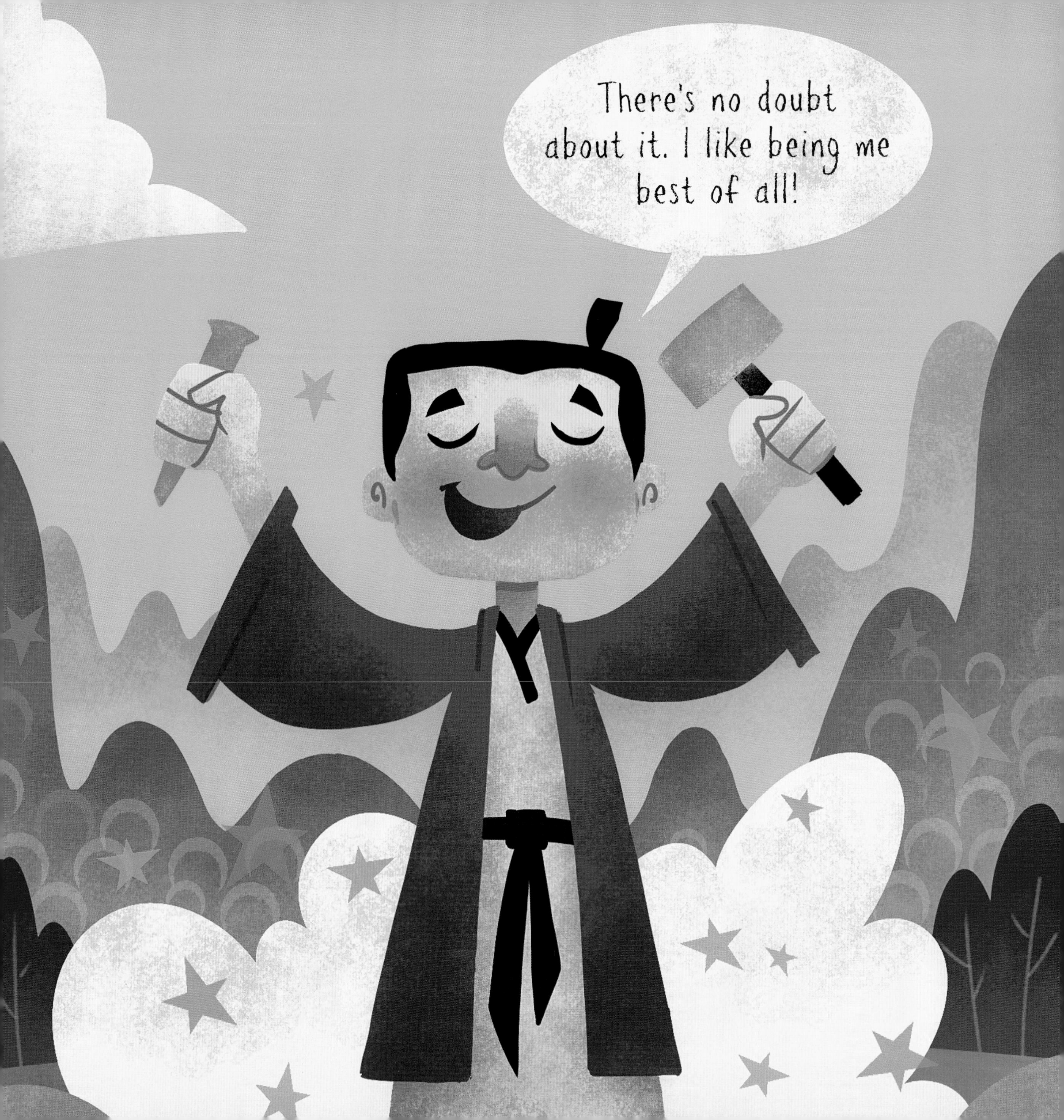
There's no doubt about it. I like being me best of all!

Jack
and the
Beanstalk

Jack and his mother were so poor, they never had enough to eat. One morning, they had nothing left at all.

"You'll have to take the cow to market and sell her," Jack's mother said sadly.

On the way, Jack met a strange little man.
"I'll give you these for your cow," said the little man,
holding out five wrinkly, dried beans.

"I need money, not beans," said Jack.

"Ah, but these are magic beans," said the little man. "If you plant them, they'll grow into a beanstalk so tall it touches the sky."

"Amazing!" said Jack. He gave his cow to the little man, took the beans and ran off home.

But when he got home
he was in trouble...
big trouble...

"Jack, we need money,
not beans!" cried his
mother, and she threw the
beans out of the window.

Poor Jack went to bed hungrier and gloomier than ever.

What were they to do?

In the morning, even his room seemed gloomy.

His *room* seemed gloomy? Just a minute...

Outside his window was a giant beanstalk,
so tall it touched the sky.

"The little man was right!" thought Jack. He scrambled onto the giant beanstalk and climbed up... and up... and up...

...and there, at the top, he found a giant castle – with a giantess in front of it!

Jack gulped... Then his tummy rumbled.

"Excuse me," he called out. "Please could you spare some breakfast?"

The giantess picked him up. "My husband munches and crunches little people like you," she said.

"I'll give you breakfast, but you'd better be gone before my husband gets home."

She whisked Jack inside, and set him down next to an enormous, crusty loaf. Breakfast had never tasted so good.

But then...

STOMP!

STOMP!

STOMP!

"Quickly, hide in here."
The giantess stuffed Jack
into a pot, just as a giant
strode into the kitchen.

Fee! Fi! Fo! Fum!
I smell the blood of an Englishman,
Be he alive, or be he dead,
I'll grind his bones to make my bread!

"Where is he?" demanded the giant,
and he started to search the table.

"You're imagining things," said his wife.
"Eat up your breakfast while I bring your hen."

She returned with the hen and put it on the table.
"Lay!" commanded the giant.

Clink!
The bird laid a gleaming golden egg.

With a grunt, the giant
closed his eyes and
began to snore.

The giantess lifted
Jack out of the pot.

"Run for your life!"
she whispered.

But Jack had his eyes
on the hen.

He grabbed the hen and fled for the door.
The bird let out a squawk

...which woke the giant,
who saw Jack and let out a furious ROAR!

Jack dived out of the door and
onto the beanstalk, with the
giant hot on his heels.

Jack scrambled down the beanstalk
as fast as his legs would carry him.

"What's going on?" shrieked his mother from below. "Is that a– a– **GIANT?**"

"Just bring the axes!" Jack cried.

Jack and his mother chopped
and chopped at the beanstalk.

It creaked and wobbled,
then it toppled over sideways.

The giant was flung
far over the hills.

They never
saw him again.

As for Jack and his mother, they lived happily ever after.

Each morning, the hen laid a golden egg, so they grew rich. And Jack never climbed another beanstalk.

The Roly-Poly Rice Ball

Miki was a poor woodcutter.
Although he worked hard,
he never had enough to eat.

One day, he woke to find nothing left
but a bowl of old, cold rice.

He scooped out the rice, squashing and squeezing, until he had made a round, roly-poly ball.

"I'll keep it for lunch," he thought.

He wrapped it up carefully.

Then, trying to
forget his hunger
pangs, he set off
into the forest.

Chop...

Chop...

Miki chopped log after log after log...

...until he couldn't ignore his tummy any longer.

Rumble-rumble

He set down his hatchet.
"Time for some food," he thought hungrily.

Oops!

But, somehow,
the rice ball slipped
from his hands.

Bump-bump-bumpity-bump! It raced down the slope and disappeared between twisting tree roots.

"No-oooo!" gasped Miki, diving after it.

He stretched out his arms...

stumbled...

Ow!

Oooh...

...and tumbled
headlong into a hole.

Ooof!

Bump! He landed deep underground. But it wasn't dark.
Strings of lanterns gave off a cheerful glow.

Miki rubbed his sore head and stared.
All around him, mice in bright silk robes
were singing and dancing.

He listened in amazement...

A roly-poly rice ball,
A roly-poly treat.

Roll away, roll away,
Here for us to eat.

"They're singing about my lunch!"

"Welcome!" squeaked the mice, when their song was finished.

Miki smiled.
"Thank you," he said.

Some of the mice were turning his rice into miniature, mouse-sized cakes.

A mouse in a red jacket scampered over.
"Will you join our feast?" he asked.

Miki nodded eagerly. "I'd love to!"

So Miki ate a rice ball feast with the mice.
And then he sang and danced with them, too...

A roly-poly rice ball, A roly-poly treat,

Roll away, roll away,

Here for us to eat.

At last, it was time to go home.

The mouse in the red jacket shook Miki's hand.
"Thank you for coming," he squeaked,
"and for sharing your rice with us."

Now we have a gift for you!

He handed Miki something small and surprisingly heavy.

Bye-ee.

It was a glittering
golden spoon.

Miki waved the spoon admiringly.
There was a swirl of golden light and...

...a bowl of fragrant, fresh-cooked
rice appeared from nowhere.

He waved the spoon again. Gold coins rained down around him, chinking and clinking onto the ground.

It must be magic!

Miki has never wanted for food or money
from that day to this – all thanks to the
magical mice and their wonderful golden spoon.

Dick
Whittington

Dick Whittington was a poor country boy.
He had no money for a warm home,
or new clothes,
or yummy food.

So he hiked up hills...

...and down dales, in search of work.

One fine morning, he met a farmer.

"I'm looking for a job," declared Dick.

Can you help me?

"Sorry, son," sighed the farmer. "Why not try London?
They say the streets there are paved with gold."

Dick's eyes lit up. "Gold!" he cried, excitedly. "I'll be rich."
And off he trotted, with a spring in his step.

He trekked...

and tramped...

and trudged.

But when he reached
London, his heart sank.

The streets weren't made
of glittering gold at all...

...just sooty old stone.

Yawn!

Exhausted, Dick flopped
down on some steps and
slipped into a deep sleep.

155

He awoke the next morning
with a start.

"Scram, scruffbag!"
shouted a woman.

"Now, now, Mrs. Grub,"
said a deep, friendly voice.
"The poor boy looks hungry."

"Would you like to come in?"
the man asked with a smile.

"My name is Fitzwarren," he told Dick. "I'm a sea trader.
I buy and sell things from all over the world."

Wow!

"You look as if you
need breakfast,"
he added.

Mr. Fitzwarren gave Dick a huge bowl of porridge.

Then he offered him a job, cleaning the kitchens.

Move it,
shorty!

Dick had to put up with Mrs. Grub,
the grumpy housekeeper – but it was worth it.

That night, a maid showed Dick to
his bedroom in the creaky attic.

My very
own room!

Dick was overjoyed. He even
had blankets to snuggle into
as he went to sleep.

Dick had hardly closed his eyes, when...

...up through
the floorboards
popped a mouse.   Then another...

...and another!

Soon, the whole room was filled with sneaky, squeaky mice.

Poor Dick didn't get a wink of sleep.

Squeak!

Squeak!

Squeak!

A week later, Dick got his first ever wages – one whole penny.

"What *shall* I spend it on?" wondered Dick, when he visited the market.

Raspberry smoothies
2 pennies

Creamy cakes
3 pennies

Rhubarb chews
1 penny

Penny whistles
(you guessed it)
1 penny

ips
each

Then he saw
the very thing.

YE PET SHOP

Kittens
1 penny

Frog starter kits
1 penny

Puppies
2 pennies

He handed over his penny and
picked up a warm, furry kitten.

"I'll call you Tom," said Dick.

"Just wait 'til those meddlesome
mice meet you!"

That night, the mice popped up as usual.
But Dick was ready for them...

The mice scurried for cover
and Dick slept soundly at last.

One morning, Mr. Fitzwarren called everyone together.

"My biggest ship is going on a trading voyage," he declared.

"If any of you have something to sell, it can go on board."

Dick only had one thing he could sell – Tom.

"Maybe someone would give me *two* pennies for him," he thought.

With a sad sigh, Dick waved goodbye to his clever kitty.

Dick missed Tom...

...especially when the mice came back.

Squeak!

Squeak!

Squeak!

Squeak!

His sleepless nights began all over again.

Dick was so tired, he began dozing off during the day.

Wake up, lazybones!

"I've had enough of Mrs. Grub's grouching," he thought.

So he decided to run away.

As dawn broke the next day,
Dick crept out of the house.

Soon he reached
the road out of
London.

As he strode along, the church bells rang out.

♪ Turn again, Whittington, thrice Mayor of London! ♪

"How strange," thought Dick. "The bells are telling me to go back...

...and they say I'll be Mayor!"

Dick returned to Mr. Fitzwarren.

"Great news, Dick!" he cried.
"A rich king bought your cat,
and Tom chased all the mice
from his palace."

Here's your
payment.

Mr. Fitzwarren handed
Dick two bulging bags of gold.

When he grew up, Dick used his gold
to become a terrific trader, like Mr. Fitzwarren.

Not only that...

...he was Mayor of London three times,

just as the bells had said!

Hooray!

Hooray for the Mayor!

The King's Pudding

Deep in the leafy green depths
of the jungle lived Little
Deer and his old enemy...

...snarling,
growling,
pouncing
TIGER!

"I'm going to EAT YOU UP!" said Tiger, one morning. "You can be my breakfast."

"You can't eat me," said Little Deer. "I'm guarding the King's pudding."

"It's the most delicious pudding in the world!"

"No one is allowed
to touch it!"

"Not even *me*?"
snarled Tiger.

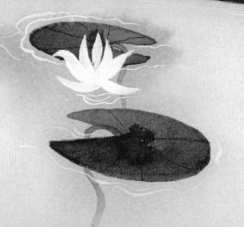

"The King would
be furious!" said
Little Deer.

"Please let me have a little
taste," begged Tiger.

"Hmm... We'll have to pretend you
chased me away," said Little Deer.

And Little Deer ran away,
singing, "I'm as clever
as can be, try and try
but you can't catch me."

Tiger opened his mouth
wide and...

"BLEURGH!"

"This isn't pudding!
It's stinky, yucky,
revolting MUD.

Just wait till I catch
you, Little Deer," he roared.

Tiger stalked through
the jungle, until at last
he found Little Deer.

"Tiger!" gasped
Little Deer.

"Lunch!" growled Tiger.

"Oh no," said Little Deer.
"I can't possibly be your lunch."

"I'm guarding the King's belt."

"The King's belt?" asked Tiger.

Little Deer pointed to a twisting, shining loop on a branch.
"No one else is allowed to touch it."

"Not even me?" snarled Tiger.

"It could be our little secret,"
said Tiger.

"Fine," said Little Deer. "Let's pretend
you chased me away."

And Little Deer ran
away as fast as he could,
singing, "I'm as clever
as can be, try and try
but you can't catch me."

Tiger draped the belt around his waist. It coiled tighter and tighter.

The belt hissed. "This isn't a belt. It's Cobra!"

Tiger ripped off the snake and
ROARED.

"Just wait till I catch you, Little Deer."

That evening, as Little Deer
drank from the river, he heard
a rustling in the bushes.

"Tiger?"
said Little Deer.

"Dinner!"
growled Tiger.

"Oh no!" said
Little Deer. "You
can't eat me."

191

"I'm guarding the King's drum."

"The King's drum?" asked Tiger.

"It's just above me,
hanging in the tree.
No one else is allowed
to touch it."

"Not even me?" asked Tiger.

"Not even you," said Little Deer.

"Unless..." said Little Deer,
"we pretend you chased me away."

And he ran away, singing,
"I'm as clever as can be, try and try
but you can't catch me."

Tiger patted the King's drum. There was a humming and a buzzing and out poured a horde of angry wasps.

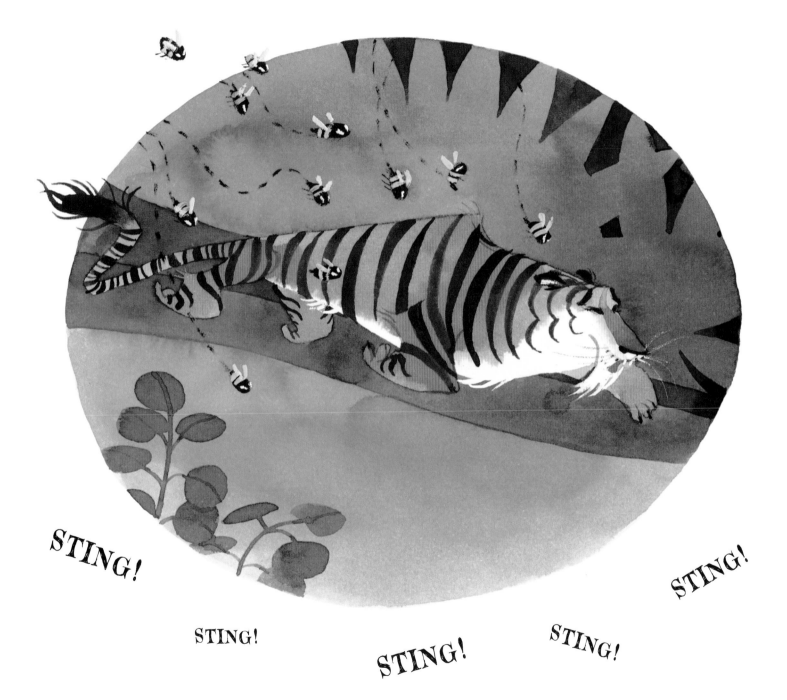

STING!

STING!

STING!

STING!

STING!

"I give up!" howled Tiger.

"I promise I'll never try to eat you again!"

Far away in the forest, Little Deer smiled, and sang,
"I'm as clever as can be, try and try but you can't catch me."

The Tin Soldier

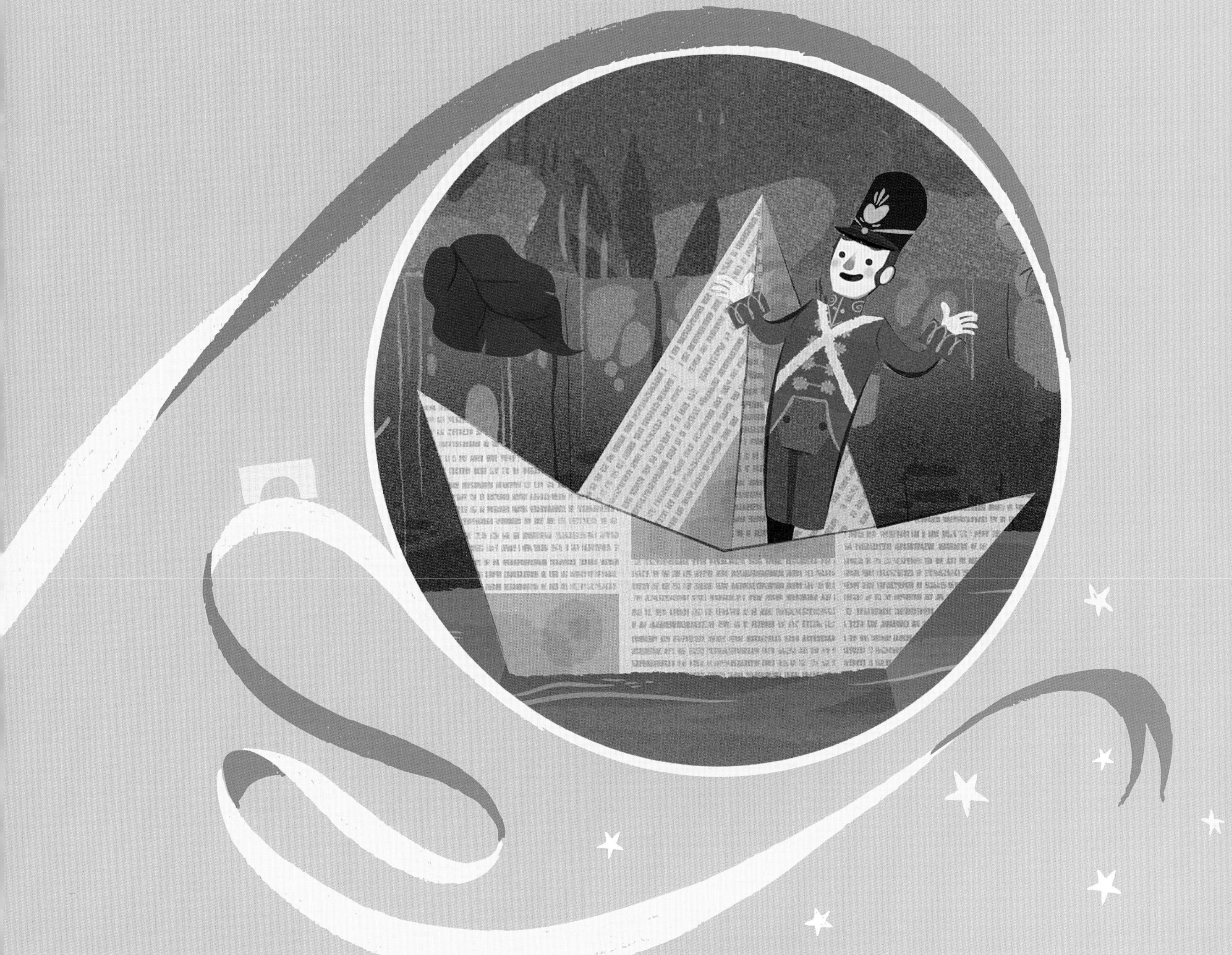

"Atten-tion!" said Tom, saluting his shiny new tin soldiers.

"Oh dear!" said Grandpa. "This little fellow only has one leg."

Tom didn't mind. He spent all day marching his troops around the house.

That night, while Tom was sound asleep,
his toys magically sprang to life.

"Whoopee!" they yelled.
"Now it's our chance to play."

But the one-legged soldier didn't want to play.
    He'd fallen head over heel in love with the paper ballerina.

He gazed in awe, as she twirled on one leg.
    "She's perfect," he thought.

"Stop staring, soldier!" snapped
the jealous jack-in-the-box.

She's mine. Stay away!

The next morning, Tom put the soldier by the window.
Up popped the jack-in-the-box.

"Look out, soldier!" hissed the
other toys, as loudly as they dared.

They were too late.

"So long, tin head!" sneered the jack-in-the-box.

Taking a deep breath,
he *blew*
the little soldier
outside.

Help!

Ha ha!

As he fell, the tin soldier was whipped up by the wind.

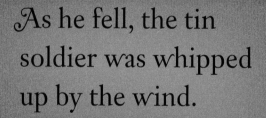

He clattered and clanged along the street.

Two mischievous boys spotted him.
"Look, a soldier!" cried one.

Let's turn him
into a sailor.

They made him a boat out of newspaper.

Enjoy your voyage!

The paper boat whirled away with the helpless soldier aboard.

"I feel seasick," thought the soldier, as his boat was swept onwards.

My poor tummy!

He was headed straight for a dark, dirty drain.

He shut his eyes and held on tight.

Whoosh! The little boat
tumbled through the hole
and landed, splat,
in a stinky sewer.

The soldier sailed on,
until he came to a filthy rat.

"Stop right there!"
snapped the rat.
"You must pay me a
penny to pass."

"Sorry," called the soldier as he floated by. "I don't have any money."

Hey, come back!

The boat fell
out of the
sewer...

Wooaah!

...and landed,
splash, in a
river.

By now, the paper boat was so soggy, it sank.

"Glug!" gurgled the soldier,
as he came face to face with a huge fish.

The hungry fish gobbled up
the soldier in one bite.

"Mmm," thought the fish.
"A bit tinny, but not bad."

But the little toy's luck
was about to change...

A fisherman caught the fish.
"What a whopper!"
he cried with delight.

The fisherman took the fish into town
to sell on his market stall.

Who should buy the fish,
but Tom's grandpa.

He took the fish home to cook for supper. But when he unwrapped it...

...out plopped the tin soldier.

Plop!

Grandpa rushed to see Tom.
"Look who I've got," he said.

"Welcome home,"
said Tom happily.

All the toys were delighted to see the soldier back, safe and sound.

Well, almost all...

"Rats!" growled the jack-in-the-box.

Grrr!

He was so angry, he bounced up and down furiously for an hour, until at last...

...his springs couldn't take any more.

Boing! went one.

Sping! went another.

With a final wheeze, the bad-tempered toy flopped over, and never worked again.

The tin soldier and the ballerina were married that very night.

"Hooray for the happy couple!" cried the other toys, and they danced until dawn.

About the Stories

Goldilocks and the Three Bears is an old fairy tale, which has been around for many years. It first appeared in a printed book in 1837, in a collection of stories by a British author named Robert Southey.

The story of **Tom Thumb** is centuries old. A booklet of his story, *The History of Tom Thumbe,* was printed nearly 400 years ago but he was a traditional character in folk tales long before that.

The Genie in the Bottle is a tale from a very old collection of stories known as *The Arabian Nights.* Some people say the King of Persia's beautiful, clever wife made up the stories to entertain him.

The Stonecutter is a traditional tale from Japan. There are lots of stories from all over the world about people who want a different life and end up back where they started.